# HOCKEY

# Morning, Noon and Night

by doretta groenendyk

The Acorn Pr
Charlottetown
2014

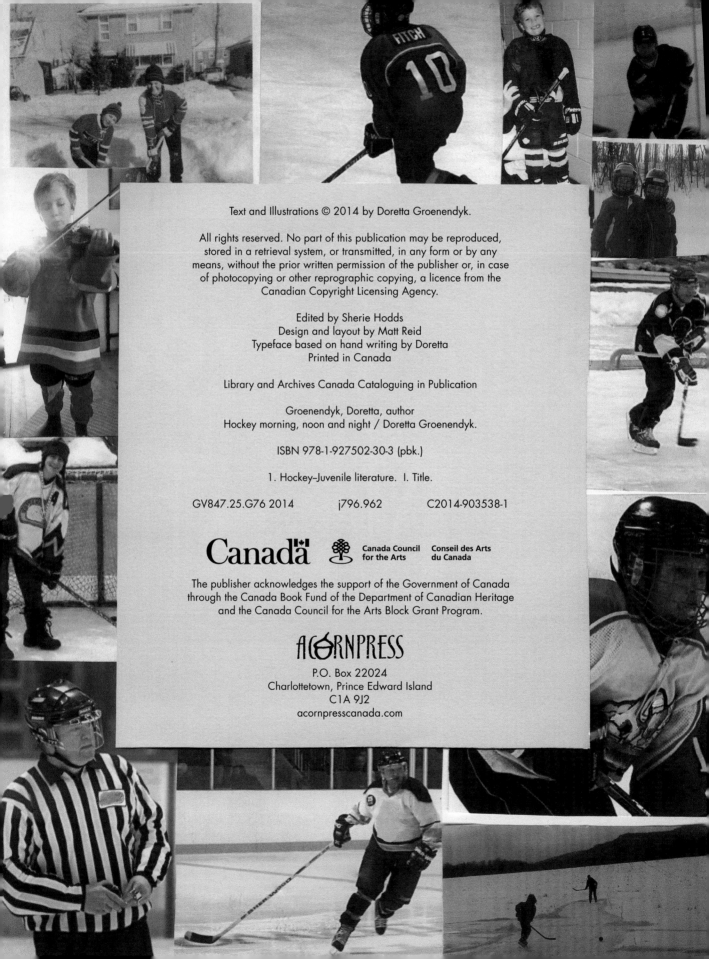

Edited by Sherie Hodds
Design and layout by Matt Reid
Typeface based on hand writing by Doretta
Printed in Canada

Library and Archives Canada Cataloguing in Publication

Groenendyk, Doretta, author
Hockey morning, noon and night / Doretta Groenendyk.

ISBN 978-1-927502-30-3 (pbk.)

1. Hockey–Juvenile literature.  I. Title.

GV847.25.G76 2014          j796.962          C2014-903538-1

Canada       Canada Council     Conseil des Arts
             for the Arts       du Canada

The publisher acknowledges the support of the Government of Canada
through the Canada Book Fund of the Department of Canadian Heritage
and the Canada Council for the Arts Block Grant Program.

ACORNPRESS

P.O. Box 22024
Charlottetown, Prince Edward Island
C1A 9J2
acornpresscanada.com

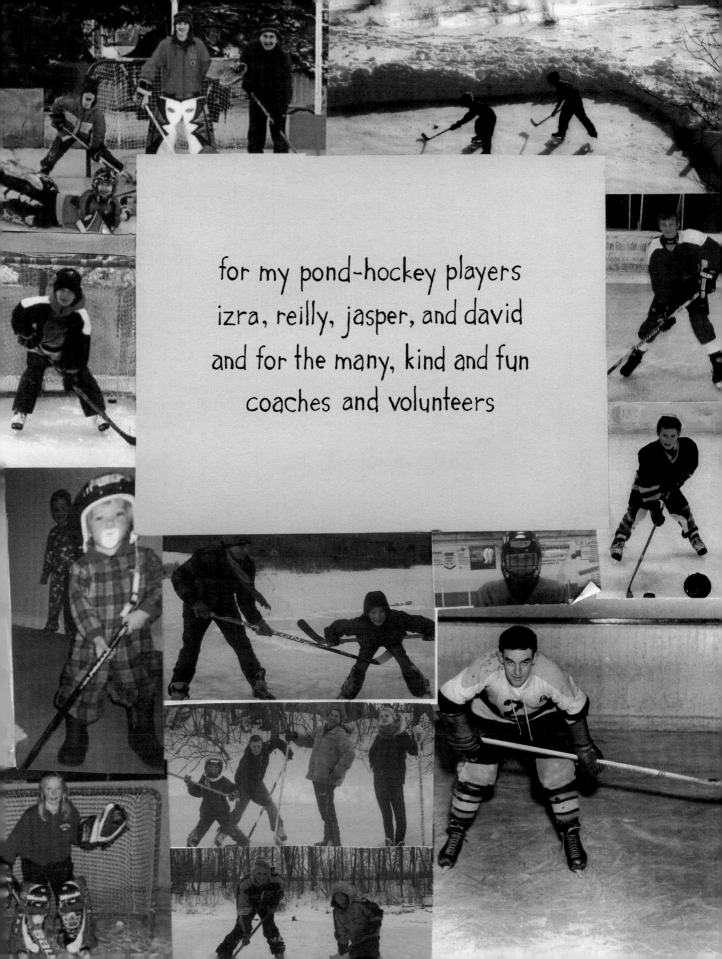

for my pond-hockey players
izra, reilly, jasper, and david
and for the many, kind and fun
coaches and volunteers

Here's our friend Pepper,
So happy and bright.
It must be the hockey,
Morning, noon and night.

He wakes up real early,
From dreams of a goal.
Pours Frosted Hockey cereal
And milk in a bowl.

He reads of his heroes
On the back of the box,
Then zips up his bag,
Full of pads, skates and socks.

He arrives at the rink,
Has a scrimmage on the ice.

He lifts the puck and skates fast,
Thanks his coach, who is nice.

All his friends love to play.
They shout their team cheer!
Then it's time for hot chocolate
While they dry their gear.

Back at home, Pepper draws
Scenes of great hockey players.
They're taped to the fridge,
All hanging in layers.

He plays mini-sticks
With his friend from next door.
Their boots are the goal posts,
And they argue the score.

They trade hockey cards
And compare the big names,
While Pepper's mom and sister
Play their own hockey games.

The Her-i-canes is their team,
And the games are intense.
His sister's the goalie,
His Mom plays defence.

Pepper dreams of playing
In an NHL game,
Hopes for 20 hat tricks,
To make the Hall of Fame.

If he can't play pro,
Pepper says with a grin,
He'll still play the anthem
On his violin.

Pepper's dad has flooded
The pond and it's great.
They put on their helmets,
Excited to skate.

Thursday they shovelled
To get the ice right.
There's **nothing** like pick-up
On the pond at night.

The neighbours join in,
All playing for fun.
Pepper shoots, doesn't score,
But still feels like he's won.

Everyone laughs,
As they skate, shoot and aim
The puck toward the net
In the final game.

It's time to head home.
Pepper's tired as can be.
In his hockey PJ's,
He finds the game on TV.

Now Pepper's fast asleep.
Third period came too late.
As he nods off,
In his dreams he will skate.

Tomorrow he'll wake,
Still filled with delight.
For Pepper loves hockey,
Morning, noon and night.